SEA T

PAUL LINSEY.

by the same author

VERSE
A Local Habitation
Selected Poems

BIOGRAPHY
Wednesday Early Closing

NORMAN NICHOLSON

Sea to the West

faber and faber
LONDON · BOSTON

*First published in 1981
by Faber and Faber Limited
3 Queen Square London WC1N 3AU*

*Printed in Great Britain by
Redwood Burn Limited, Trowbridge, Wiltshire and
bound by Pegasus Bookbinding, Melksham, Wiltshire.
Reprinted 1987
All rights reserved*

© *Norman Nicholson 1981*

*This book is sold subject to the condition that it shall not, by way of
trade or otherwise, be lent, re-sold, hired out or otherwise circulated
without the publisher's prior consent in any form of binding or cover
other than that in which it is published and without a similar condition
including this condition being imposed on the subsequent purchaser*

British Library Cataloguing in Publication Data

Nicholson, Norman
Seat to the west.
I. Title
821'.9'14

ISBN 0-571-11745-7
ISBN 0-571-11729-5 (Pbk)

To my wife
in love and gratitude for
TWENTY-FIVE SILVER YEARS
1956–1981

A poet's hope: to be,
like some valley cheese,
local, but prized elsewhere

W. H. AUDEN, *Epistle to a Godson*

Acknowledgements

The author is grateful to The Ceolfrith Press, Sunderland, for permission to include the six poems previously printed in *Stitch and Stone* (with illustrations from embroideries by Kenneth Dow Barker, 1975), and to Mid-Nag Publications, Ashington, Northumberland, for fourteen poems from *The Shadow of Black Combe* (1978). Also to *Country Life* for 'Comprehending It Not', and to Macmillan, London, for 'Weeds', which first appeared in *Young Winter's Tales No. 5*. 'Weeds' was also issued by Mid-Nag Publications as one of their Poetry Posters. 'Hard of Hearing' is printed by permission of the Poem of the Month Club; 'The Cathedral' was written to celebrate the 900th anniversary of the foundation of Winchester Cathedral; 'The New Cemetery' first appeared in *My Britain*, published in aid of Oxfam by Oxford University Press.

Thanks for certain poems are also due to the editors of the following: *Hibernia* (Dublin), the *London Magazine*, *New Poetry* (Workshop Press), *New Poetry 5* (Arts Council anthology, Hutchinson), *Outposts*, *Phoenix*, *Poetry Review*, *The Times Literary Supplement*, *Words 7*.

Finally, the author gratefully acknowledges assistance from the Arts Council of Great Britain during the time he was working on the poems in this collection.

Contents

Scafell Pike	page 11
Beck	13
Wall	15
Cloud on Black Combe	17
The Shadow of Black Combe	19
Black Combe White	20
Clouded Hills	21
Shingle	22
Dunes	24
Tide Out	26
Plankton	28
Sea to the West	30
Weeds	31
Toadstools	33
Haytiming	35
Nobbut God	36
The Cathedral	37
Fjord	39
Glacier	41
Midsummer Fires on the Sognefjord	43
Cornthwaite	45
Landing on Staffa	46
Glen Orchy	48
On the Dismantling of Millom Ironworks	49
The Bloody Cranesbill	51
Comprehending It Not	53
Hard of Hearing	55
At the Musical Festival	57
Do You Remember Adlestrop?	58
'Is There Anybody There?' Said the Traveller	59
The Safe Side	60
The Register	61
The New Cemetery	62
Halley's Comet	64

Scafell Pike

Look
Along the well
Of the street,
Between the gasworks and the neat
Sparrow-stepped gable
Of the Catholic chapel,
High
Above tilt and crook
Of the tumbledown
Roofs of the town—
Scafell Pike,
The tallest hill in England.

How small it seems,
So far away,
No more than a notch
On the plate-glass window of the sky!
Watch
A puff of kitchen smoke
Block out peak and pinnacle—
Rock-pie of volcanic lava
Half a mile thick
Scotched out
At the click of an eye.

Look again
In five hundred, a thousand or ten
Thousand years:
A ruin where
The chapel was; brown
Rubble and scrub and cinders where
The gasworks used to be;
No roofs, no town,
Maybe no men;
But yonder where a lather-rinse of cloud pours down
The spiked wall of the sky-line, see,
Scafell Pike
Still there.

Beck

Not the beck only,
Not just the water—
The stones flow also,
Slow
As continental drift,
As the growth of coral,
As the climb
Of a stalagmite.
Motionless to the eye,
Wide cataracts of rock
Pour off the fellside,
Throw up a spume
Of gravel and scree
To eddy and sink
In the blink of a lifetime.
The water abrades,
Erodes; dissolves
Limestones and chlorides;
Organizes its haulage—
Every drop loaded
With a millionth of a milligramme of fell.
The falling water
Hangs steady as stone;
But the solid rock
Is a whirlpool of commotion,
As the fluid strata
Crest the curl of time,
And top-heavy boulders
Tip over headlong,
An inch in a thousand years.
A Niagara of chock-stones,
Bucketing from the crags,
Spouts down the gullies.
Slate and sandstone
Flake and deliquesce,

And in a grey
Alluvial sweat
Ingleborough and Helvellyn
Waste daily away.
The pith of the pikes
Oozes to the marshes,
Slides along the sykes,
Trickles through ditch and dub,
Enters the endless
Chain of water,
The pull of earth's centre—
An irresistible momentum,
Never to be reversed,
Never to be halted,
Till the tallest fell
Runs level with the lowland,
And scree lies flat as shingle,
And every valley is exalted,
Every mountain and hill
Flows slow.

Wall

The wall walks the fell—
Grey millipede on slow
Stone hooves;
Its slack back hollowed
At gulleys and grooves,
Or shouldering over
Old boulders
Too big to be rolled away.
Fallen fragments
Of the high crags
Crawl in the walk of the wall.

A dry-stone wall
Is a wall and a wall,
Leaning together
(Cumberland-and-Westmorland
Champion wrestlers),
Greening and weathering,
Flank by flank,
With filling of rubble
Between the two—
A double-rank
Stone dyke:
Flags and through-
stones jutting out sideways,
Like the steps of a stile.

A wall walks slowly.
At each give of the ground,
Each creak of the rock's ribs,
It puts its foot gingerly,
Arches its hog-holes,
Lets cobble and knee-joint
Settle and grip.
As the slipping fellside
Erodes and drifts,
The wall shifts with it,
Is always on the move.

They built a wall slowly,
A day a week;
Built it to stand,
But not stand still.
They built a wall to walk.

Cloud on Black Combe

The air clarifies. Rain
Has clocked off for the day.

The wind scolds in from Sligo,
Ripping the calico-grey from a pale sky.
Black Combe holds tight
To its tuft of cloud, but over the three-legged island
All the west is shining.

An hour goes by,
And now the starched collars of the eastern pikes
Streak up into a rinse of blue. Every
Inland fell is glinting;
Black Combe alone still hides
Its bald, bleak forehead, balaclava'd out of sight.

Slick fingers of wind
Tease and fidget at wool-end and wisp,
Picking the mist to bits.
Strings and whiskers
Fray off from the cleft hill's
Bilberried brow, disintegrate, dissolve
Into blue liquidity—
Only a matter of time
Before the white is wholly worried away
And Black Combe starts to earn its name again.

But where, in the west, a tide
Of moist and clear-as-a-vacuum air is piling
High on the corried slopes, a light
Fret and haar of hazy whiteness
Sweats off the cold rock; in a cloudless sky
A cloud emulsifies,
Junkets on sill and dyke.
Wool-end and wisp materialize
Like ectoplasm, are twined
And crocheted to an off-white,
Over-the-lughole hug-me-tight;
And Black Combe's ram's-head, butting at the bright
Turfed and brackeny brine,
Gathers its own wool, plucks shadow out of shine.

What the wind blows away
The wind blows back again.

The Shadow of Black Combe

In wise, proverbial days they used to say
That everybody born
Under the shadow of Black Combe
Will come back there to die.

                        Come
Back Arthur, come back Andy, come back Will.
Come home,
While there's still time.

And all you who were shot in France,
Drowned in the Great Lakes,
All exiles and dole-day migrants,
Who swallowed influenza, took T.B. like snuff—
Get ready to come back. Once
Is not enough.
Get ready to die again.

There's room for you
Under that sprawled, green burial mound,
Under the round,
Turfed, cobble-dashed dome,
Herring-bone masonry of slivered stone,
Where a crag-fenced, shovelled-away entrance
Gill cracks back
To some before-man-made cavern, some
Ordovician catacomb—
For you,
For all the thousand millions of the earth,
Black Combe has room.

But as for me,
I'm staying here,
Not leaving it to chance—
One death will do for me.

Black Combe White

Sixty-mile drive to a reading—arriving by dark,
The audience sparse, the room unsuitable,
And bed in a cold hotel. At 8 a.m.
I draw the curtains, and there, beyond the roof-tops,
Bulging from the flat ledge of the horizon
Like a blister on the white paint of a window-sill,
Black Combe—its unmistakable cleft forehead,
No bigger than a thimble now, outlined in chalk
On the blue distemper of the sky. I turn from the cold
To a room grown more welcoming than before:
'It's been snowing at home!' I say.

                                        Sixty mile back,
Edging the ooze of the estuary mosses—sheep
One side on fire from the level sun; hedges
Clinkering ginger; every dyke and mole-hill
Casting an acre of shadow. And soon
From each rise in the road, each break in the hills' barrier,
Comes glimpse after glimpse of the nearing Combe, first white,
Then patchy, and then streaked white on black,
Darkening and sharpening every minute and every mile.

Home at last to the known tight streets,
The hunched chapels, the long canals of smoke—
And now, from my own doorway, between gable and chimney,
That harsh, scarred brow, entirely stripped of snow,
Impending over yard and attic sky-light,
A dark, parental presence. And when the neighbours tell me:
'The Combe was white last night!'—I don't believe them.
It's always black from here.

Clouded Hills

Though you can't see them,
You know that they are there.

Beneath the Herdwick fleece of mist,
You can feel the heave of the hill.

You can sense the tremor of old volcanoes,
Tense with damped-down fire.

Under a white meringue of cumulus,
Or behind the grey rain-break of a winter's day,

You are aware of the pikes straining high above you,
Spiking up to an unseen sky.

Shingle

It surges down—
Slow underpull
Of heavy grey waves,
Meeting the sea's
Surge upwards.

Never a backflow, always
This crawl of a fall.
On the line of the swell
Each long crest crumbles
Into a sud of stone
Medallions and ovals,
Smooth as butterbeans;
But the shoulder of the wave
Is cumbered with cobbles
The size a stone-waller
Might pile into a barn.

At the bank's bottom step
The obtuse-angled
Thrust of the tide
Shovels the pebbles
Inwards and slant-wise,
For the surf to suck back again
The breadth of a winkle-shell
From where they were before.

A mounded migration
Of crab-backed stones,
Tide by tide, moves
Sideways along the shore.

But here at the highest
Rung of the rise—
A gull's stride under
The shivering overhang
Of sea-spurge and marram—
Only the wildest
Tides arrive
To dump sacks of boulders
On the shrivelled wrack,
Where the stones reside
A while on their circuit,
Inch by inch
Rolling round England.

Dunes

The waves of the sea
Flood up the staggered shore,
Pour along fanned-in runnels,
Slap splashily on flabby jetties;
At the prod of the equinox
They clamber over parapets, wriggle under garden gates,
Scrabble among fuchsias and pebbles,
Batter at sand-bagged doorways,
Savage buckets and brushes and a child's forgotten shoe;
With a frothing of bladderwrack
They bluster and topple
And ebb back to the strand.
The waves of sand
Flood, swell, impend,
And do not ebb at all.

The dunes stalk the town,
Month by month stretching an extra ripple,
A brown reinforcing roll.
They are shovelling the warrens out of the front street;
They are sweeping the foreshore from the window-sills.
Backyard elders and sheds and allotment fences
Stand swamped to the knees in the dry silicic flood,
And litter-bins lie buried to the collar.

Away on the hawes the turf rebukes the dunes.
The waves of sand subside, the yellow swell
Calms to a green trough.
Rest-harrow, bedstraw and the wiry dyer's greenweed
Fit a wickered raft of raffia
Along the trapped tide—the moon's pull

Can magnet scarcely a grain above mean sand level.
In the neap of the day the natterjack toad
Occupies an urgent, emergent terrain
Of slithery hillocks and furrows and finger-nail screes.
The spiked marram's springy knitting-needles
Purl and entangle what concrete cannot conquer
And the green holds back the brown.

Plant, then, the green, plant marram, plant buckthorn;
Let sea-holly not be uprooted;
Entrench the town behind a fortified zone of grass.

For landward from the horizon the waves of the sea
Flood and ebb,
Flood and ebb,
But here on the verge of the surge the waves of sand
Flood, swell,
Poise themselves, and,
For a little while,
Stay still.

Tide Out

Ebb-tide at sunset:
    the last light
Slides up the channel
    as the sea slides down.
Shadows tunnel
    level into an elevated
Atlantis of sand.
    The day's green aftermath
Seeps along ginnel
    and dried-up canal.
Sahara on Sahara,
    brown ripples of dune
Recede in metallic
    low relief,
And glimmering, salty
    tea-spoon oases
Simmer and mirage
    in the frothing dusk.
The filter-feeders
    burrow back into the mud;
Mussel and barnacle
    bar their trap-doors.
Walnut-shell worm-casts
    lean east into umbra,
And the Poor Man's Weather-glass
    accepts its hour of air.
Here in the wide
    inter-tidal lull
The estuary suffers
    a Pleistocene age of change.
A night's storm
    recontours a continent;
Sand-slide and canyon
    dissect the exposed plateau.

The tide returns
> to a never-before-visited
Up-thrust and eroded world,
> arid as mica—
World of the wind's shaping and dead
> sand-grain avalanche—
Till, prompt on the tick
> of moon-clock time,
The oxygenated brine
> drowns it back into life.

Poor Man's Weather-glass: *Laminaria saccharina,* one of the brown sea-weeds or kelps.

Plankton

The great un-living energies
Tug at the earth's
Fluid overcoat,
Shake it like a blanket.
The moon applies brakes
And the volts spark off.
The battering wet
Battery of waves
Flashes sheet lightning
And the tides thunder
Under a ninety-
Million-mile-off sun.

But inches below
The enveloping film
Between brine and vapour,
The lesser energies
Explode into self-propulsion—
Single cells
Developing fins,
Tentacles, tails;
A tiny octopus,
Rayed like the sun,
That moves as the sun can't.

The earth turns its neck
And the sun exits;
And, dead on the dark,
The sea's cuticle
Phosphoresces with life,
Glows with the fry
And minutiae
That build up the body of the whale.

Dawn
Hatches out a spawn of glitter.
A bacterium
Becomes aware of itself,
Hears its own echo.
As the white day
Climbs up the sky,
The lesser energies,
From a billion billion
Microscopic eyes,
Look back at a blind sun.

Sea to the West

When the sea's to the West
The evenings are one dazzle—
You can find no sign of water.
Sun upflows the horizon;
Waves of shine
Heave, crest, fracture,
Explode on the shore;
The wide day burns
In the incandescent mantle of the air.

Once, fifteen,
I would lean on handlebars,
Staring into the flare,
Blinded by looking,
Letting the gutterings and sykes of light
Flood into my skull.

Then, on the stroke of bedtime,
I'd turn to the town,
Cycle past purpling dykes
To a brown drizzle
Where black-scum shadows
Stagnated between backyard walls.
I pulled the warm dark over my head
Like an eiderdown.

Yet in that final stare when I
(Five times, perhaps, fifteen)
Creak protesting away—
The sea to the west,
The land darkening—
Let my eyes at the last be blinded
Not by the dark
But by dazzle.

Weeds

Some people are flower lovers.
I'm a weed lover.

Weeds don't need planting in well-drained soil;
They don't ask for fertilizer or bits of rag to scare away birds.
They come without invitation;
And they don't take the hint when you want them to go.
Weeds are nobody's guests:
More like squatters.

Coltsfoot laying claim to every new-dug clump of clay;
Pearlwort scraping up a living between bricks from a ha'porth
    of mortar;
Dandelions you daren't pick or you know what will happen;
Sour docks that make a first-rate poultice for nettle-stings;
And flat-foot plantain in the back street, gathering more dust
    than the dustmen.

Even the names are a folk-song:
Fat hen, rat's tail, cat's ear, old men's baccy and Stinking Billy
Ring a prettier chime for me than honeysuckle or jasmine,
And Sweet Cicely smells cleaner than Sweet William though she's
    barred from the garden.

And they have their uses, weeds.
Think of the old, worked-out mines:
Quarries and tunnels, earth scorched and scruffy, torn-up
    railways, splintered sleepers,
And a whole Sahara of grit and smother and cinders.

But go in summer and where is all the clutter?
For a new town has risen of a thousand towers,
Every spiky belfry humming with a peal of bees.
Rosebay willow-herb:
Only a weed!

Flowers are for wrapping in cellophane to present as a bouquet;
Flowers are for prize arrangements in vases and silver tea-pots;
Flowers are for plaiting into funeral wreaths.
You can keep your flowers.
Give me weeds.

Toadstools

October is springtime
For mushrooms and toadstools,
For mole-hill rings
Of Parasol, Snow Bonnet,
Ink Cap and Death Cap,
Beef-steak and burnt-out
King Alfred Cakes.
You may not care a rap
What name each takes,
But eat the wrong one
And you'll soon know you've done it.
Flitters and off-comes
Of ground-damps and dews;
Chlorophyll-lackers,
Slackers and shirkers,
Puff-lumps with no green
Blood in their veins;
Plants that toil not,
That never learn to
Earn their daily
Crumbs of sun;
White octopus-threads,
Under bark, under soil,
That suck dear death
Out of petal and frond,
With never a summering,
Never a giving
Of pollen or seed—

But a parasite-toll
On the whole green set-up.
There are more species
Of moulds and fungi
Than of all the flowering
Plants of the earth—
And the flowers, under lowering
Back-end skies,
Dying, admit:
It's one way of living.

Haytiming

'It's late so soon,' he said—
The sun still high but the day nearly over,
The weed at July and summer toppling.
Away in the intake,
The scaled-out grass sprawled sodden, the ewes wanted clipping,
And the lambs were as big as their mothers.
He stared across the dale.
On its eastern shoulder every cobble and clint
Was seven-times magnified under a lens of light;
The other slope was plunged in a reservoir of shadow.
Bracken, rank and viscous, stank like compost,
The rowans were already reddening,
And the rag-mat of autumn lay coiled up in the corries,
Waiting to be rolled out over fell-foot and byre.
He pushed segged thumbs through hair too early grey,
And said again: 'That's the trouble with summer—
It's late so soon.'

Nobbut God

> *First on, there was nobbut God.*
> Genesis, *Chap.* 1, *v.1.*, *Yorkshire Dialect Translation.*

First on
There was silence.
And God said:
'Let there be clatter.'

The wind, unclenching,
Runs its thumbs
Along dry bristles of Yorkshire Fog.

The mountain ousel
Oboes its one note.

After rain
Water lobelia
Drips like a tap
On the tarn's tight surface-tension.

But louder,
And every second nearer,
Like chain explosions
From furthest nebulae
Light-yearing across space:
The thudding of my own blood.

'It's nobbut me,'
Says God.

The Cathedral

They built the great cathedrals
By laying stone on stone:
They built *this* one
By taking stone away.

Take away the grey
Weathered outcrop, the glint of crystal,
Black heather and yellow pepper
And rowan, up its lithe hose-pipe
Gushing green into blue;
Take away the fell walls,
Slate-slab roofings, tile-hung frontages,
And the worn flagstones of a farm kitchen;
Take away the rock and all that comes out of the rock—
And what you're left with
Is this hollow quarry
We call 'The Cathedral'.

Said the old philosophers
Of the Negative Way:
There is no road to God
Through the landscape of man's imaginings.

Forget
All you've ever thought of;
Forget rock and sky;
All human mediation
Of finger, lip and eye;
Objects, ideas of objects,
Ideas of ideas;
Forget everything that God is not—
And what you're left with
Will be no further from what God is
Than this hollow quarry
Is from the built splendour
We call a cathedral.

'The Cathedral' is the name given to a huge cavern in an abandoned slate quarry near Little Langdale in Cumbria.

Fjord

This ice-scoop, this
Sunk valley,
Drowned inwards from the sea
As a reed-deep pool
Drains back into a ditch.
A buzzard flies
Above the waveless water-line
Not half so high
As fish swim far
Below it.
        Here
The pop-eyed crawlers
Of barely post-glacial ooze
Climb miles up a steep bank
To gain the sea's hard floor.
                         Here
A chartered cruise-ship
Edges up to the quay
As lenses tighten
On wharf and wooden church and waterfall.
A gull or two
Take noisy notice; a dog
Rolls in the gravel track beside the shore;
And the ship slides off again
To New York or Majorca,
Trailing a wake
That rakes no deeper than a chain-harrow
The lake's brittle surface.

But fathoms below
That five-minute ripple,
Below the plankton's arable, the mapped
Approach-route of the salmon,
Far deeper than the shelf
That underpins Norway and the Shetlands,

The locked-in water
Lies still as a rock—
While calculable tides
Roar and storm round the northern latitudes—
Holds its cold
A degree above freezing,
A day's thaw from the last
Dead millennium's calendar of ice.

The fjord's glass veneer
Glows bottle-green all night;
Stars find
Hardly enough dark to shine in;
The clock clicks
Twenty-three day-lit
Bewildering hours.
But drop your watch in that water
And when it touches bottom
It will tell yesterday's time.

Glacier

Its hectares of white
Out of sight from below,
It gropes with one green paw
The rim of the rock-fall.
Each claw
A crunching of bottle-glass,
Opaque and raw,
Splinters as big as a cottage
Cracked between tongs:
A malevolent, rock-crystal
Precipitate of lava,
Corroded with acid,
Inch by inch erupting
From volcanoes of cold.

Slow
Paws creak downwards,
Annexing no
Extra acreage of stone—
For each hooked talon
Is pruned back and pared
By mid-June sun,
And a hundred sluicings
Ooze down the inclined plane
To a wizened, terminal
Half-cone of snow.

The ebb and flow
Of becks that live for a minute
Swishes bath-salt icebergs
Through a shingle moraine—
Where the dandy, grey-rust
Fieldfare rattles
Pebbles in its crop,
And the dwarf cornel
Blinks like a black-eyed buttercup
On the brink of the milk of melting.

Summer now
Out-spills the corrie
With a swill of willow,
But winter's overhang
Retreats not a centimetre—
No fractured knuckle, no
Refrigerated bone
Relinquishes grasp,
Lets slip a finger-hold
To the bland noon's seepage.

For behind black
Rock-terraces and tiers
Slumped winter waits—
For a tilt of earth's axis,
A stretching-out of the polar cold,
To restore the normal, to correct
The climate's misdirection,
Corroborate and order
Mean average temperature
For the last million years.

Midsummer Fires on the Sognefjord

No sunset, no onset of the dark. The eleven-hour-
Long afternoon dims to a hesitant evening.
Overflow pipes from unseen waterfalls
Go on generating electric power;
The glacier greys into cloud; the sea eases almost tideless fingers
    Among the ribs of fells

So named in our Cumbrian tongue, inherited from these
Voes, viks, fosses and mosses. Down by the white
Verandah'd hotel, children enact their fake folk-wedding.
Tourists converse in German and Japanese.
Away on the fjord the oil-can raft burns brighter
    Downwards in the water, while outside wooden

Boat-house and shed, each family lights its fire-sign,
Flapping one to the other like flags along the swing of the shore.
The track through the orchard slowly fills with midnight.
Acres of elder and pale breakers of keck drift white on the dusk's
    brine;
And the map of the puckered coast-line is dirtied over
    To the vague guess of a Vinland chart.

And now, at the day's lowest dip, from aluminium-
Smelting towns, creviced in creeks, and from holiday hutments
    seen
Not even by noon, huge bonfires bore
Tunnels through the mist; a spark lit a millennium
Ago floats up from unchronicled darkness, flies westward towards
the brown
    Ebb-flowing of the year.

And, maybe, five months from now and the North Sea's
   width away,
I'll watch that spark catch light on a Cumbrian slagbank,
Where boys put matches to heaped sleepers and old bicycle tyres,
And crackers contradict the blacking out of day,
And a smoulder of cardboard and privet exhales, acrid and rank,
   Faint reek of ancestral fires.

Cornthwaite

Cornthwaite, 'the clearing of the corn',
My mother's maiden name—whose umpteenth great-grandfather,
Off-come from a northern voe, hacked thorn,
Oak-scrub and birch from rake and beck-bank
To sow his peck of oats, not much of a crop.
Lish as a wind-racked larch, he took his trod
Through landscape nameless still to him, until,
Remembering his own grandfather's talk
Of *tveit* and *dal* and *fjell*,
He scratched those words on the rocks,
Naming the Cymric cwms in a Norse tongue.
The land then named him back.
And here, a millennium later, my baptismal card
Clacks echoes of a clearing beneath cracked
Granite and black pines, where the migrant fieldfare breeds
And the ungregarious, one-flowered cloudberry
Is commoner than crowding bramble. Now,
In my own day's dale, under the slant
Scree of unstable time, I lop,
Chop and bill-hook at thickets and rankness of speech,
Straining to let light in, make space for a word,
To hack out once again my inherited thwaite
And sow my peck of poems, not much of a crop.

Landing on Staffa
or
REGULARITY

      Said
Sir Joseph Banks in 1772,
  en route for Iceland,
'Where now is the boast of the architect!
  REGULARITY,
the part in which he fancied to exceed
  his mistress, Nature,
is here found in her possession, and here
  has been for ages
undescribed.'—His observations, quoted
  in Pennant's *Tour of*
Scotland and Voyage to the Hebrides,
  brought the describers:
Scott, Keats, Wordsworth, who found the ground crowded
  ('each the other's blight,
hurried and hurrying'); Sir Robert Peel,
  wide brow bared before
'temple not made by hands'; F. Bartholdy-
  Mendelssohn, weaving
wave-shape and cave-shape in quavers—and me
  at a loss for words.
Images proffer themselves—a grooved chip-
  potato cutter,
a wash-tub rubbing board, rolled cordduroy,
  the corrugated
iron of a Calvinist Methodist
  chapel, crunched pillars
'bound together like a bunch of matches'
  (Keats said), or ploughed fields
fossilized and up-ended—a dozen
  such knick-knack conceits.

The columns crack into hexagonal
   stools of black basalt;
islands float sweetly, heads scarcely above
   water—the Dutchman
drowned in the Celtic tangle, his hat left
   drifting on the swell.
Mull and Ulva heave like basking seals and
   the tide slides backward.
But the air is blurred with words; pencillings,
   shadings, engravings,
drape huge fish-nets between see-er and seen.
   Quick eyes are dimmed by
a cataract of known appearances.
   The sky pales to a
green familiar aquatint. In the year
   1847,
the Queen and Prince Albert entered the cave
   and haunt it yet. I
turn from the sky-lit gallery, the praised
   portfolio of
A Hundred Famous Views, scurrying south,
   down the ragged rip
of the tartan, to grey unphotographed
   waste acres of West
Cumberland. There, in dark claustrophobic
   winter, I retrace
lonnings once-known to the feet of childhood:
   streets, pavements, schoolyards,
railings, allotments, fields undermined and
   sunken, or horse-tailed
sumps on the flank of a crumbling pit-bank:
   seeking still to find
one ten-yard panorama, broken fence,
   brown cast-iron tree,
criss-cross curve of slag and slanted grass, or
   just one single stone
that must have lain for ages undescribed—
   and then describe it.

Dutchman's Hat: a small island off the coast of Mull, visible from Staffa.

Glen Orchy

Sunday, late summer, 1968:
Mull and Iona behind me and eleven days
Of Highland brightness—Loch Awe electro-plated,
Ben Cruachan chiselled and faceted like cut-glass
In a cubic clarity of air; the River of Orchy,
Subterranean almost, glittering below
Hollowed and pendant shelves of sandy stone.
And everywhere down crag and brae, a tumbling
And cataract of yellowing green, birch and rowan,
Leaf and berry and the churned froth of heather.

                                                   Then,
Passing through the village at the foot of the glen,
I stop at a shop with newspapers for sale
And take one, glancing for the cricket scores—
When, like a snapped spring, a familiar name
Headlines clean at me: 'Millom Ironworks
To Close in Four Weeks Time'.

                                     And now,
Whenever I remember Glen Orchy,
I see the stretch of light, the waterfalling seasons,
And ten thousand years of after-Ice-Age weathering
Crash on an Arras Wood of smokeless furnace chimneys,
And, blundering among the dead trunks, five hundred men
At one stroke out of work.

On the Dismantling of Millom Ironworks

> *Child of the clouds! remote from every taint*
> *Of sordid industry thy lot is cast.*
> William Wordsworth, *The River Duddon*, ii

I laughed once at those words—for there, near where he pondered
On Duddon Bridge, shallow-draft barges shot their ore,
Even in Wordsworth's day, for the charcoal-burning furnace
Sited like a badger's set deep in Duddon woods.
Twenty years on, at the river's mouth, the Hodbarrow miners
Kicked up mountainous mole-hills; a conifer copse of chimneys
Criss-crossed the west with spikes and laterals, and landslides of
  limestone
Walled off all sight of the tide. The river seeped from the
  marshes
In a flux of haematite. Today, two lifetimes later,
Bled white of every stain of ore, the Duddon rediscovers
Its former channel almost unencumbered—mines
Drowned under stagnant waters, chimneys felled and uprooted,
Slagbanks ploughed down to half their height, all cragginess,
Scrag-end and scree ironed out, and re-soiled and greened over
To long sulky drumlins, dumped there by the look of them
An ice-age ago. They cut up the carcass of the old ironworks
Like a fat beast in a slaughter-house: they shovelled my childhood
On to a rubbish heap. Here my father's father,
Foreman of the back furnace, unsluiced the metal lava
To slop in fiery gutters across the foundry floor
And boil round the workmen's boots; here five generations
Toasted the bread they earned at a thousand degrees Fahrenheit
And the town thrived on its iron diet. On the same ground now
Split foundations moulder in the sea air; blizzards
Of slag-grey dust are blown through broken Main Gate uprights;
Reservoir tanks gape dry beside cracked, empty pig-beds;
And one last core of clinker, like the stump of a dead volcano,
Juts up jagged and unblastable. Stand on the rickety pier,
Look left along the line where gantry and crane and coke-bank

Ten years ago blocked all the view—and now you're staring
Bang at Black Combe. The wind resumes its Right of Way;
Shelduck fly low from feeding-ground to feeding-ground,
No intervening chimneys forcing an upward flight.
In parallel troughs, once dug for the long-since-rotted sleepers
That carried the rails to the tip, cardboard and tags of sacking
Accumulate mulch for dockens and shunting-yards succumb
To a yellow encroachment of ragwort. The town shrinks and
    dwindles.
Old People's Bungalows creak half-way up the hill,
Over a mile away, and privet hedge and hydrangea
Screen out even the memory of smoke and slag. An age
Is pensioned off—its hopes, gains, profits, desperations
Put into mothballs. A hundred years of the Bessemer process—
The proud battery of chimneys, the hell-mouth roar of the
    furnace,
The midnight sunsets ladled across a cloudy sky—
Are archaeological data, and the great-great-great-grandchildren
Of my grandfather's one-time workmates now scrounge this iron
    track
For tors and allies of ore bunkered in the cinders and the hogweed.
And maybe the ghost of Wordsworth, seeing further than I can,
Will stare from Duddon Bridge, along miles of sand and mud-
    flats
To a peninsula bare as it used to be, and, beyond, to a river
Flowing, untainted now, to a bleak, depopulated shore.

The Bloody Cranesbill

Every Sunday morning, when I was ten or twelve,
My father and I set off and called on my Uncle Jim
For the weekly fraternal walk. Five minutes' talk with my Auntie,
Then through the allotments, the playing-field, the lonning, out
To the links and warrens and foreshore of the already dying mine
That yet had thirty more years of dying to live through. No longer
The bustle and clang of my father's apprentice days—a thousand
Boots reddening the road at the end of the morning shift:
A Sabbath Day quiet now, no sound but the ricochet,
On the vast, glass, railway-station roof of sky, of the chuff and splutter
Of one single locomotive, straining at the week-by-week
Ever-steepening gradient of a hill of unsaleable ore.
The metals undulated bumpily over hillock and hollow
Like a fairground roller-coaster; screes of ore
Dustbinned on to rusty willows; the romanesque brick pit-head
Towers of Number Ten now and then twirled their wheels,
Lifting a couple of miners or half a ton of ore.
We scuffed through a scabbed and scruffy valley of ruddled rocks
To Cumberland's southernmost point, a headland, half-blasted-away,
Where the limestone met the tide. Here, on the seaward side,
Wave-action moulds the rocks, thumbs them like plasticine;
Landward the crag splits vertical down to the old workings.
We traversed the yard-wide col between quicksand and quarry, and there,
In a cockle-shell dip in the limestone, matted with thrift and rock-rose,
Was Sunday's flower, the Bloody Cranesbill, red as the ore
It grew from, fragile as Venetian glass, pencilled with metal-thread
Haematite-purple veins. The frail cups lay so gently

On their small glazed saucer-bracts that a whisper would have
   tipped them over
Like emptying tea-leaves out. Every Sunday morning
I bent and picked one flower and every time it withered
Before we were half-way home to my Uncle Jim's. Fifty years
   later,
And it's hard to tell there ever was a mine: pit-heads
Demolished, pit-banks levelled, railway-lines ripped up,
Quarries choked and flooded, and all the lovely resistance
Of blackberry, blackthorn, heather and willow grubbed up and
   flattened.
A barren slack of clay is slurried and scaled-out over
All that living fracas of top-soil and rock. A town's
Purpose subsides with the mine; my father and my Uncle Jim
Lie a quarter of a century dead; but out on its stubborn skerry,
In a lagoon of despoliation, that same flower
                    Still grows today.

The Bloody Cranesbill, *Geranium sanguineum*, is fairly common at a number of places on the Cumbrian coast.

Comprehending It Not

December, 1921. Seven years of age,
And my mother dead—the house in mourning,
The shop shut up for Christmas—I
Was fobbed off to my Grandma's with my Christmas Tree
Bundled under my arm. Out
In the brown packed streets the lamplight drizzled down
On squirming pavements; the after-smell of war
Clung like a fungus to wall and window-sill,
And the backyards reeked of poverty. Boys,
Their big toes squirting through their boots,
Growled out *While Shepherds Watched* to deaf door-knobs,
And the Salvation Army—euphoniums, slung, unplaying—
Stumped the length of the town at the thump of a drum
To cracked Hallelujahs in the Market Square.

I edged past muttering entries, sidled inside the lobby,
And slammed the door on the dark. My Grandma
Banged the floor with her stick to greet me,
Tossed me a humbug and turned again to the goose,
Spluttering on the kitchen range. My four rough uncles
Barged jokily around in flannel shirtsleeves,
Challenged to comic fisticuffs or gripped me
With a wrestler's grip and hyped me and cross-buttocked
In Cumberland-and-Westmorland style—till puffed, at last, and weary
Of horse-play and of me, they ripped my Christmas
Tree from its wrapper, unfolded its gaunt
Umbrella frame of branches, stuck candles in the green raffia,
And stood it on the dresser, well out of my reach.

I crouched down by the fire, crunching my humbug,
And scissoring holly and bells from coloured card;
The huff of the smoke brought water to my eyes,
The smell of the goose made me retch. Then suddenly,
The gas plopped out and the house was doused in darkness—

A break in the main and not a chance of repair
Till the day after Boxing Day. Matches rattled;
A twist of paper torn from the *Daily Mail*
Relayed the flame from grate to candle,
And soon, high on the dresser, my Christmas Tree,
Ignited like a gorse-bush, pollened the room with light.

Proud as a proselyte,
I stuffed white wax in the mouth of a medicine bottle,
Pioneered the wild lobby and the attic stairs
And dared the heathen flagstones of the yard,
Bearing my gleam of a gospel. At the scratch of a match,
Christmas crackled up between winter walls,
And Grandma's house was home, her sharp voice called in
    kindness,
And the fists no longer frightened. Tickled at the trick of it,
I 'Merry-Christmased' gas-pipe, gas and gas-men,
'God-blessed' the darkness and pulled crackers with the cold—
Scarcely aware what it was that I rejoiced in:
Whether the black-out or the candles,
Whether the light or the dark.

Hard of Hearing

The landscape of sound
Grows slowly dimmer.
A hush simmers
Up from the ground.
Words are blurred; vowels
Lose almost all their colour;
The lipped and tongued sharp edges
Are smudged and sponged away,
And in an aural darkness
All voices look alike.

Ears staring
Under the twilight,
I grope and blunder
My way to a meaning.
Through the slithering dusk
Walk stumbling, eyes
Strained to the south-
west linger of day.

For behind gloomed tree-trunks
And in shadowy doorways
Unspeaking faces
Gape blankly about me.
Night ties
Bandages round my ears:
Turns verbs
To Blind Man's Buff;
Sends me to black
Coventry in my own skull,
Where not one crack
Of light breaks in
From the town's genial hubbub.

For not from out there
Will come my brightening:
Not from that other dumbness.
Myself is my only
Lamplighter now.
I must illumine my own silence,
Give speech to the blank faces;
If the town won't talk,
Must put words in its mouth.

At the Musical Festival

'He gev it Wigan!' we'd say long ago
When our loved local baritone,
Rendering *The Erl King* or *Ruddier than the Cherry*,
Hurled his voice like an iron quoit
Clean into the Adjudicator's
Union-Jacked box at the back. Never mind
If he was out of tune or muddled his words
Or finished bars ahead of the accompanist—
He'd won his marks, he'd done
What he set out to do; he'd
Given it Wigan.

                The map of England
Was a small one then. London
Was Wembley; Blackpool was holidays;
Manchester was the Test:
All else, a blurred and hachured diagram
Of dialects and geology. We chose
Our bench-marks and points of reference within day-return
Of the one place we knew. It was
Barrow for ships, Whitehaven for coal,
Millom, of course, for men,
And Wigan for a damned good try.

So when, apprehensively, I
Go up for my last class and adjudication—the hall packed,
The audience tense, the examining pencil
Slanted on the unmarked sheet—then,
As I huff and grate and fill my lungs, and eye
The once-for-all starting bell,
God grant me guts to die
Giving it Wigan.

Do You Remember Adlestrop?

Someone, somewhere, must have asked that question—Robert
Frost, may be, or Abercrombie, or, that now
Forgotten genius, John W. Haines, who scarcely
Wrote a line himself but knew the knack
Of making others write them. Someone
Who called at Steep that cold January, '15,
The poet laid up in bed with a sprained ankle—and 'Yes,
Yes, Yes!' he shouted, as the happy accident
Unsnecked the trapdoor of his memory,
'And willows, willow-herb, and grass'
Burgeoned from a compost of fermenting words—
'Yes, Yes, Yes!' and now everyone remembers.

Is there no question
To fork air into my long-dormant root-stock? No
Fag-card flash of a boy's bright slagbank day,
The wild barley in the back street, the quite impossible catch
That snatched the match and the cup? The questions come,
Blunt and bullying as a bad conscience,
But always the wrong ones.—'Do you remember
Stoke Newington, Stockport, Crewe or Solihull?'—
And sadly, guiltily, I reply: 'I'm sorry'—
The trapdoor banged down tight, the compost sour and black—
    'No'—
Not even sure if I've ever been there—
'No, I don't remember.'

'Is There Anybody There?' Said the Traveller

I called on my friend in the evening;
   I knocked at the front door.
Three thuds thumped along the lobby—
   No sound more.

No light at the front windows.
   I went round to the back,
Found the rear door open,
   Pushed through to the black

Steep-walled chasm of the kitchen-yard;
   Stumbled on roots
Of Virginia Creeper creeping
   From up-ended chimney-pots.

I groped my way to the window,
   Stood stock-still
While a faint wash of firelight
   Oozed over the window-sill.

I tapped on the glass of the window:
   For answer, not a sound.
But the firelight like a goldfish
   Kept skittering round and round.

It glittered along the shelves of books,
   Titles, to me, unknown,
And down on the black and dizzy wax
   Circling on the gramophone.

And I heard then a hushed conversation,
   Fellow to fellow:
Falsetto chitchat of two flutes,
   The aye-aye of a cello.

And I turned and blundered down the dark,
   Heels scraping backyard loam—
'Mustn't interrupt', I said:
   'Bach's at home.'

The Safe Side

'It's better to be on the safe side,' my father used to say,
Picking up an umbrella when there was scarcely a cloud in the wide
Shop-window of the sky. Now, wearing his greyness, I
Lean on my wordy counter, totting up dots and commas,
Expounding that much and this much if not exactly twice
Yet rather more than once—to be on the safe side.

The Register

Wanting my Birth Certificate and not finding it handy,
I called at the Registry Office for proof that I'd been born,
And the clerk unclasped a volume and pushed it across the table:
'Perhaps you'd like to look at your father's signature?'

Two entries on each page—name, date and parents,
And the Registrar's endorsement: 'Henry Frankland Fox'—
Whose grand-daughter, now my doctor, will maybe one day
Endorse my Death Certificate and clasp up the book with a clang.

Familiar beyond all question, yet not what I'd expected,
A recognized unrecognition faded bluely on the page:
Not a father's and yet a father's, a name that perplexed and
    perturbed me,
Faces and loyalties emerging blurred from a boy's dead world.

It was the hand of James Sharpe, Bachelor of Science,
    Headmaster,
Flourished on each term's report from my twelfth to my
    seventeenth year—
Notifying there, in that last, still almost Edwardian winter,
A daughter's birth a few days before or after mine.

Two strict sergeants of my boyhood, guides, guardians,
    reprimanders,
One loved but not respected, one respected but not loved—
I held their parade-grounds apart, kept one ear for each one's
    instructions,
And their annual Speech-Day meeting wrapped embarrassment
    round the Prize.

As I stand in my father's old shop, among books he could not
    have unpuzzled,
And the hundred yards to the school lead a million miles away,
As the town my mind still lives in crumbles dustily around me—
Joseph Nicholson, James Sharpe, which one am I accountable to?

The New Cemetery

Now that the town's dead
Amount to more than its calculable future,
They are opening a new graveyard

In the three-hedged field where once
Horses of the L.M.S. delivery wagons
Were put to grass. Beside the fence

Of the cricket-ground, we'd watch
On Saturday afternoon, soon after the umpires
Laid the bails to the stumps and the match

Had begun. They'd lead them
Then between railway and St George's precinct—huge
Beasts powerful as the steam

Engines they were auxiliary to:
Hanked muscles oscillating slow and placid as pistons,
Eyes blinkered from all view

Of the half-acre triangle of green,
Inherited for Sunday. But once they'd slipped the harness,
And the pinched field was seen

With its blue lift of freedom,
Those haunches heaved like a sub-continental earthquake
Speeded up in film.

Half a ton of horse-flesh
Rose like a balloon, gambolled like a month-old lamb;
Hind legs lashed

Out at inoffensive air,
Capsized a lorryful of week-days, stampeded down
Fifty yards of prairie.

We heard the thump
Of hoof on sun-fired clay in the hush between
The bowler's run-up

And the click of the late
Cut. And when, one end-of-season day, they lead me
Up through the church-yard gate

To that same
Now consecrated green—unblinkered and at last delivered
Of a life-time's

Load of parcels—let me fling
My hooves at the boundary wall and bang them down again,
Making the thumped mud ring.

Halley's Comet

My father saw it back in 1910,
The year King Edward died.
Above dark telegraph poles, above the high
Spiked steeple of the Liberal Club, the white
Gas-lit dials of the Market Clock,
Beyond the wide
Sunset-glow cirrus of blast-furnace smoke,
My father saw it fly
Its thirty-seven-million-mile-long kite
Across Black Combe's black sky.

And what of me,
Born four years too late?
Will I have breath to wait
Till the long-circuiting commercial traveller
Turns up at his due?
In 1986, aged seventy-two,
Watery in the eyes and phlegmy in the flue
And a bit bad tempered at so delayed a date,
Will I look out above whatever is left of the town—
The Liberal Club long closed and the clock stopped,
And the chimneys smokeless above damped-down
Furnace fires? And then will I
At last have chance to see it
With my own as well as my father's eyes,
And share his long-ago Edwardian surprise
At that high, silent jet, laying its bright trail
Across Black Combe's black sky?